USBORNE SCIENCE ACTIVITIES

Helen Edom and Kate Woodward

Designed by Radhi Parekh, Jane Felstead,
Diane Thistlethwaite and Mary Forster

Illustrated by Simone Abel

Contents

SCIENCE WITH
WATER

Consultant: Frances Nagy

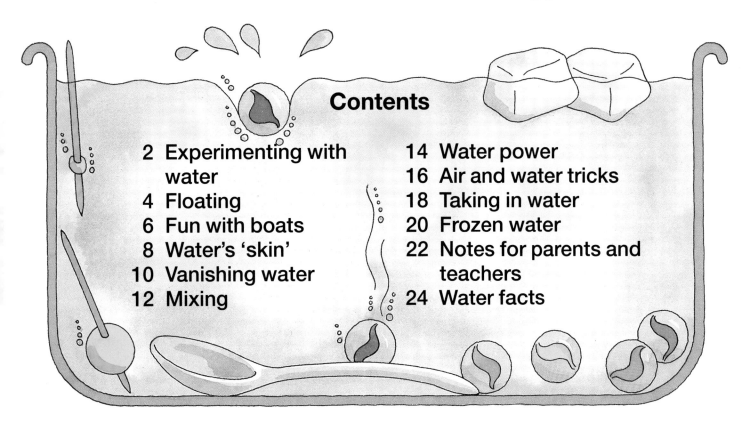

Contents

Experimenting with water

Water behaves in some surprising ways. These experiments will help you find out about them.

Things you need

You can do all the experiments with everyday things. Here are some useful things to collect.

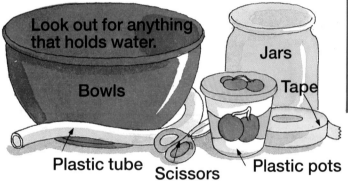

Look out for anything that holds water.

Bowls

Jars

Tape

Plastic tube

Scissors

Plastic pots

Being a scientist

Read what you have to do carefully. See if you can guess what might happen before you try an experiment.

Watch closely to see if you were right. Write or draw everything you notice in a notebook.

Science Notebook

Changing shape

Try doing these things to start finding out about water.

Pour water on some hard ground outside. Pour more water into a small jar. Does the water make the same shape?

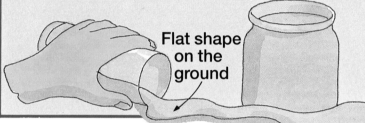

Flat shape on the ground

Looking at the top

Lid on bottle

Level table

The top of the water goes level like a table-top.

Try gently shaking a bottle half-full of water. What happens to the top, or surface, of the water? Let the bottle stand. What happens to the top now?

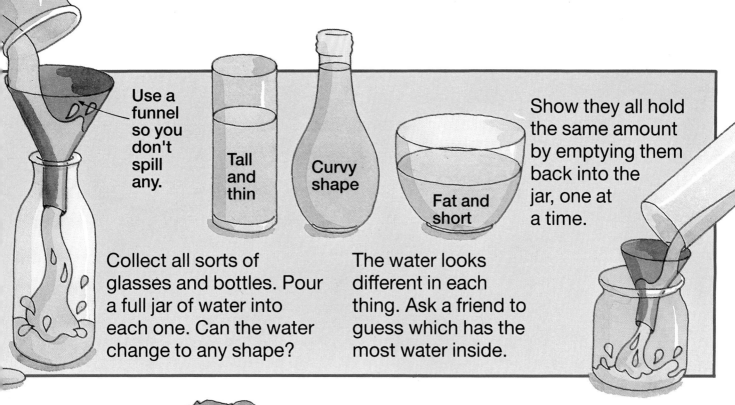

Use a funnel so you don't spill any.

Tall and thin

Curvy shape

Fat and short

Show they all hold the same amount by emptying them back into the jar, one at a time.

Collect all sorts of glasses and bottles. Pour a full jar of water into each one. Can the water change to any shape?

The water looks different in each thing. Ask a friend to guess which has the most water inside.

Rest the bottle on books to keep it steady.

Sloping bottle

Level top

Level table

What do you think will happen if you tilt the bottle? Can you make the top of the water slope? Try it and see. Check the top against a level table.

Now bend a clear plastic tube* into a U-shape. Hold it under a tap to get water inside. Is the top of the water at the same height (level) on both sides?

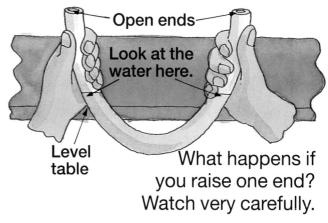

Open ends

Look at the water here.

Level table

What happens if you raise one end? Watch very carefully.

*You can buy this cheaply from a hardware shop.

3

Floating

Some things float on water while others sink.

Which things float?

Collect some things to test for floating. Can you guess which ones float before you put them in water?

Make a chart to show your results.

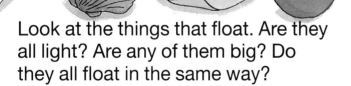

	Floats	Sinks
Cork	✓	
Tea-spoon		✓
Can		

Look at the things that float. Are they all light? Are any of them big? Do they all float in the same way?

Guess what happens if you attach a thing that floats to one that sinks.

4   *Plastic modeling clay.

Underwater floating

Attach some plasticine* to a cocktail stick to make it float upright. Add more until it sinks.

Take off a little at a time. Can you make the stick float just under the surface?

Pushing power

Try pushing a blown-up balloon into a bucket of water. It is hard to do. The water seems to push back.

What happens if you let go?

See how the water rises up the side of the bucket as the balloon pushes it aside.

Changing shape

Drop a ball of plasticine in some water. Does it float?

Flatten the ball and shape it like a boat with high sides. Does it float now?

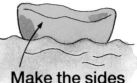

Make the sides higher if it sinks.

Testing shapes

Why does the plasticine float when you change its shape? Try this to help you find out.

Use a felt-tip pen to mark the water-level in a glass of water.

Use a wide glass.

Drop in a ball of plasticine. The water rises a little as the ball pushes it aside. Mark the new level.

First water-level

New water-level

Shape the ball into a boat and float it on the water. Why does the level rise higher?

Level for boat
Level for ball

First water-level

How it works

The boat-shape takes up a bigger space than the ball so it pushes more water aside.

The same amount of plasticine takes up more space.

The more water is pushed aside, the more it pushes back. It pushes the boat so hard that it floats.

Metal ships

Metal ships are very heavy. They are shaped so they push away a lot of water. The water pushes back hard enough to keep the ship afloat.

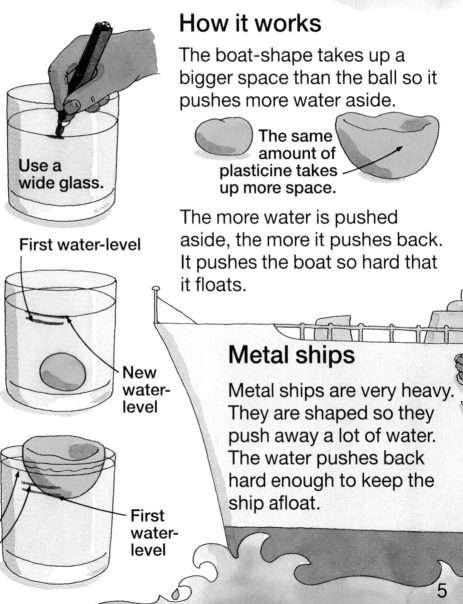

5

Fun with boats

Boats float so well that they can carry heavy things across water.

Everything that a boat carries is called its cargo.

Loading boats

Think of some things which might make good boats. You can see some here. Try them out on water.

Load your boats with a cargo of stones or marbles. Can some carry more than others?

Margarine tub boat

Boat shaped from foil.

Matchbox boat

Is it easier to push a boat-load of cargo along the ground or on the water? Try it to see.

Meat tray

Try loading a plastic meat tray with marbles. What happens?

Load some marbles into a plastic egg box. What happens if you put them all at one end?

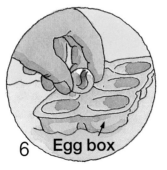

Try putting one marble in each cup-shape. Does it float better like this?

Egg box

Cargo ships

Cargo ships have dividing walls inside. This makes sure the cargo cannot move around and tip the ship over.

Sinking boat

Stick plasticine under a jar so it floats upright. Put a mark at the waterline. Load marbles gently into this boat. What happens to the mark?

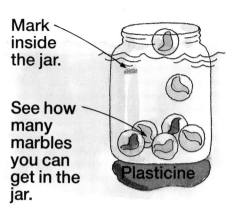

Mark inside the jar.

See how many marbles you can get in the jar.

Plasticine

Put lots of salt in the water. Float the jar now. Does the water come up to the same mark? Can the jar carry more marbles?

Plimsoll line

There are different lines for fresh and salt water.

Plimsoll line

Large boats have marks called Plimsoll lines.
People stop loading a boat when the water comes up to this mark.

Submarine can

Push an empty drink can underwater so it fills with water and sinks.

Poke one end of a plastic tube into the can. Blow into the other end. What happens?

The air you blow into the can pushes out the water. This makes the can lighter so it rises to the surface.

Air pocket   Air in

Water out

Submarines

Tanks inside a submarine can be filled with water to make it sink. Air is pumped into the tanks to make the submarine rise again.

Water's 'skin'

Here are some surprises about the top, or surface, of water.

Bulging glass

Fill a glass to the brim ▶ with water. Look closely at the top of the water. Gently slide in some coins, one at a time.

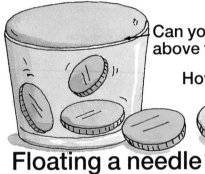

Can you see the top rise above the glass?

How many coins can you put in before the water overflows?

Pond skaters

Insects called pond skaters can walk across the top of ponds. They are so light they do not break the water's 'skin'.

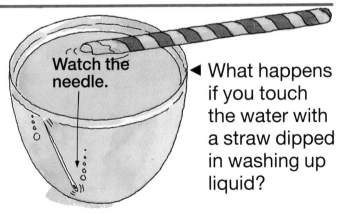

Pond skater

◀ The top of the water seems to bulge as if it is held by a thin skin. The surface of water often behaves like a skin.

Floating a needle

You can float a needle by placing it carefully on the 'skin' like this.

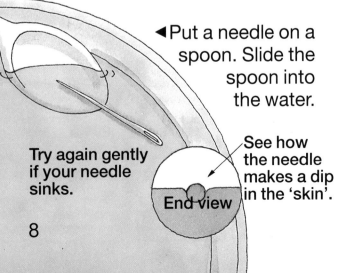

◀ Put a needle on a spoon. Slide the spoon into the water.

Try again gently if your needle sinks.

See how the needle makes a dip in the 'skin'.

End view

Watch the needle.

◀ What happens if you touch the water with a straw dipped in washing up liquid?

The washing up liquid makes the skin weaker so it stretches. It gets too stretchy to hold up the needle.

Drips and drops

Look out for drops left behind after a rainstorm. Can you guess why water stays in drop shapes?

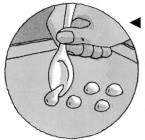

◄ Try catching a drop from a dripping tap.

Now roll it gently ► between your finger and thumb.

What shape are drops as they fall?

Can you change a drop's shape?

All drops are held by water's skin. This holds them even when they change shape.

Flattening drops

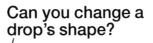

◄ Spoon some drops on to a clean plastic tray. Can you think of a way to make the drops flatter?

Try touching them ► with a straw dipped in dishwashing liquid.

The dishwashing liquid makes the skin stretch so the drops spread out.

Blowing bubbles

Stir a spoonful of water into three spoonfuls of dishwashing liquid. This mixture has a very stretchy skin.

Bend some wire into a loop. Dip it in the mixture.

Wire loop

Look at the skin across the loop. Blow gently. Watch how the skin stretches to make a bubble.

9

Vanishing water

You may have noticed how puddles dry up after rain. Have you ever wondered where the water goes?

Finding out

You might think the water just soaks into the ground or runs away. Try an experiment to see if this is true.

Pour some water into a saucer. Use a felt-tip pen to mark a line just above the water.

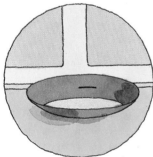

Leave the saucer on a table for a few days. Look at your mark and the water-level every day.

The water slowly vanishes. It cannot run out or soak through the saucer. It must get out another way.

How water 'vanishes'

The water escapes into the air in tiny drops called water vapor. They are too small to see.

This shows water vapor evaporating from a saucer.

This is how a puddle dries up.

Which dries fastest?

Fill three more saucers. Leave one in a cool, shady place, one in a warm place and one in a drafty place. Do they all dry out just as quickly?

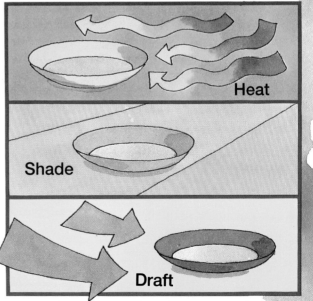

Heat

Shade

Draft

Water in the air

The way water escapes into the air is called evaporation. Water evaporates all the time from rivers and seas so the air is full of invisible water vapor.

Getting water back

Fill a jar with ice-cubes to make it cold. Does anything happen to the outside of the jar?

Wipe it with a dry tissue. Does the tissue get damp?

Put on a lid.

Water drops form on the jar because the cold jar cools the air nearby. When water vapor in the air cools, its drops get big enough to see. This is called condensation.

Steam

Sometimes condensation happens in mid-air. Then the drops look like mist. This happens when water boils.

The water gives off hot water vapor. This cools as it meets colder air and turns to drops you see as steam.

Never touch steam as it can burn you badly.

Clouds and rain

Clouds are also made up of condensation drops. These form when water vapor rises from the ground and meets cold air above.

Drops in the cloud join up and get heavier. Then they fall as rain.

Everlasting seas

Although water evaporates from seas they never dry up. Enough rainwater runs into them to keep them full.

11

Mixing

Water mixes well with many different things. To find out more about the way water mixes, first collect some jars.

Pour some water into each jar. Add a different thing to each one.

You could try: soap powder, sand, salt, flour, sugar, shampoo, cooking oil, powder paint, orange juice, jelly.

Guess what might happen to each thing before you put it in.

Does anything change if you put the same things into warm water?

Does the color change?

Put your fingers in to see if the mixtures feel like plain water.

Do any of the things you put in disappear?

Does the water get cloudy or look clear?

Write everything that does happen in your notebook.

Does it make a difference if you stir the mixtures? Watch what happens.

Science notebook

Separating mixtures

Try to think of ways to separate mixtures.

Oil floats so you can scoop it out with a spoon.

Does this work with any other mixtures?

Oil and water mixture

You could use a paper towel like a fine sieve. First fold the kitchen paper in fourths. Pull open one side to make a cone.

Put the cone in a funnel. Try pouring the sand mixture into it.

Bits of sand are trapped.

Water passes through tiny holes in the paper.

Can you separate other mixtures like this?

Solutions

Some things mix so well that you cannot separate them by scooping or sieving. A mixture like this is called a solution.

Separating solutions

Salt water is a solution. Put a drop on a saucer. Leave it until the water evaporates (see pages 10-11).

What is left behind? Taste it and see.*

Can you separate other solutions like this?

Instant food

Many foods are partly made of water. Soup, milk and potatoes are often dried and stored as powder.

When people want to eat them they just mix them with water again.

*Never taste things unless you know that they are things you can eat. 13

Water power

Water nearly always flows downhill. Its flow can push things strongly.

Make a model water wheel

You need:
2 plastic egg boxes,
2 small cardboard plates,
a stapler, some scissors,
2 empty thread spools,
a pencil, 2 long rulers or
flat sticks, plasticine,
and cellophane tape.

Can you get the wheel to turn faster?

What happens if you pour from higher up?

How does the water turn the wheel?

Cut cups* out of the egg boxes. Staple them on to one plate as shown. Staple the second plate on to the other side of each cup.

Stapler

Push the pencil through the center of the plates. Then push the thread spools on to the ends of the pencil.

Attach the rulers in place with plasticine.

Tape a ruler below each reel. Place the rulers across a bowl. Pour water on the wheel and watch what happens.

14   *You may not need all the egg-cups.

Powering machinery

Long ago people used water wheels to turn machinery for grinding wheat into flour.

Water mill

Today water is used to power machines that make electricity. The water spins huge wheels called turbines to make these machines work.

Electric generator

Turbine

Electricity is made like this in hydro-electric power stations.

Getting stronger

◄ Take the top off an empty squeeze bottle*. Make three holes in the bottle, one above the other.

Use a ball-point pen.

◄ Tape over the holes. Fill the bottle with water. Then rip the tape off quickly.

Watch how jets of water spurt out. Which goes furthest?

The lowest jet should go furthest as water above it helps to push it out.

Get an adult to help you take the top off.

Powerful pipes

Pipes to hydro-electric power stations take water from the bottom of lakes or reservoirs. The deeper the pipes are, the faster the water flows along them.

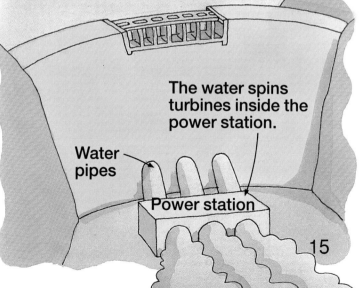

Reservoir

The water spins turbines inside the power station.

Water pipes

Power station

15

Air and water tricks

Most things that look empty are really full of air. Water has to push the air out before it can get in them.

Tissue trick

Do you think you can keep a tissue dry underwater? Try this.

First, stuff the tissue tightly into a glass so it cannot fall out.

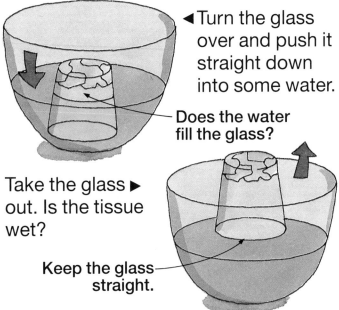

◄ Turn the glass over and push it straight down into some water.

— Does the water fill the glass?

Take the glass ▶ out. Is the tissue wet?

Keep the glass straight.

This works because the glass is full of air. The water cannot push the air out so the tissue stays dry. What happens if you tilt the glass?

Magic pot

Find an empty plastic pot with a tight lid. Use a drawing pin to make holes in its base.

Take off the lid and push the pot underwater. Now put the lid on.

What happens when you lift the pot up?

Air tries to get in the holes. It pushes so hard the water cannot get out.

Does any water fall out?

Now push a ball-point pen through the lid to make another hole. This lets air in at the top. The air helps to push the water out below.

What happens if you put your finger over the hole?

Flowing upward

Can you make water flow upward?

1. Stand a glass in the ▶ kitchen sink. Put one end of a plastic tube in the glass. Put the other end under a tap to fill the glass.

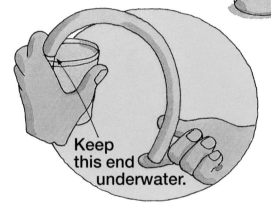

Keep this end underwater.

◀ 2. Put your finger over the top of the tube to keep the water in. Lift the glass up on to the draining board with your other hand.

3. Bend the tube until your finger ▶ is lower than the glass. Take your finger off.

The water should run up out of the glass through the tube. Can you think why?

Keep trying if this does not work the first time.

This is called a siphon.

How the siphon works

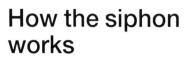

As water runs down the tube it pulls up more water behind it. Air helps to push the water into the tube so the siphon keeps flowing.

Air pushes here.

Water runs up the tube.

Water runs out here.

19

Taking in water

Some things soak up water while others keep water out.

Wetting different things

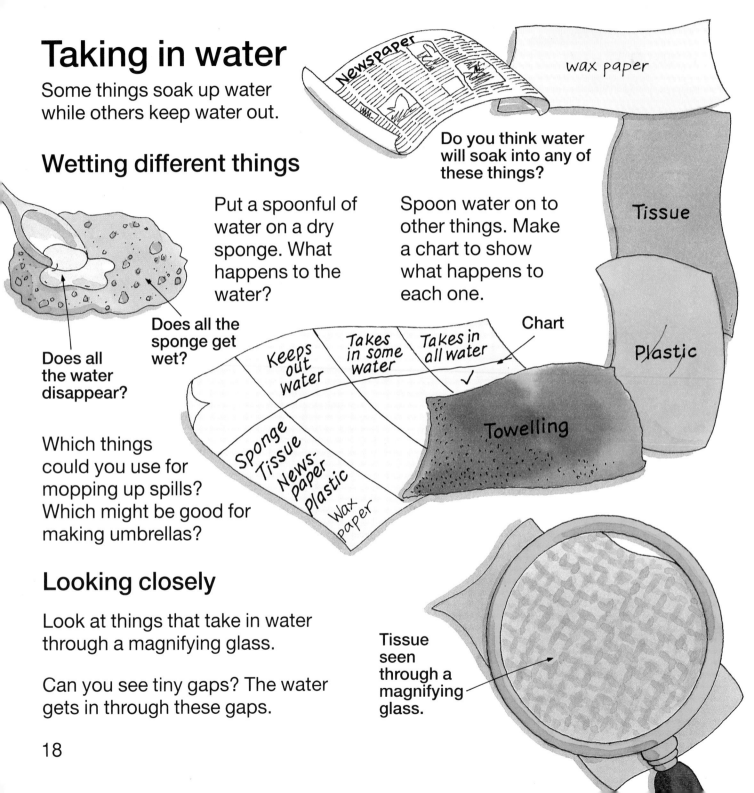

Put a spoonful of water on a dry sponge. What happens to the water?

Does all the water disappear?

Does all the sponge get wet?

Do you think water will soak into any of these things?

Spoon water on to other things. Make a chart to show what happens to each one.

Which things could you use for mopping up spills? Which might be good for making umbrellas?

Chart

	Keeps out water	Takes in some water	Takes in all water
Sponge			✓
Tissue			
News-paper			
Plastic			
Wax paper			

Newspaper

wax paper

Tissue

Plastic

Towelling

Looking closely

Look at things that take in water through a magnifying glass.

Can you see tiny gaps? The water gets in through these gaps.

Tissue seen through a magnifying glass.

Rising water

Do you think water can climb upward?

Dip a paper towel into some water. Watch what happens.

Climbing through celery

Pour a few drops of ink into a glass of water. Cut the end off a stalk of celery. Look at the cut edge closely.

Cut edge

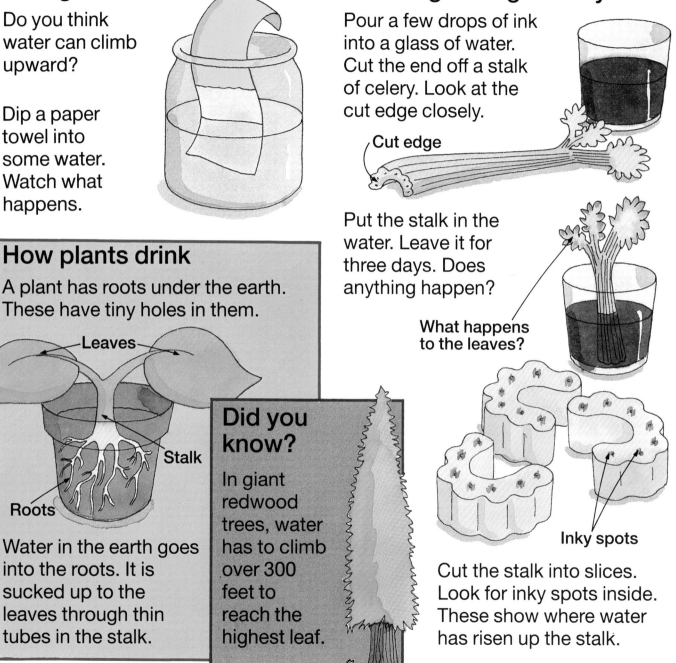

Put the stalk in the water. Leave it for three days. Does anything happen?

What happens to the leaves?

How plants drink

A plant has roots under the earth. These have tiny holes in them.

Leaves

Stalk

Roots

Water in the earth goes into the roots. It is sucked up to the leaves through thin tubes in the stalk.

Did you know?

In giant redwood trees, water has to climb over 300 feet to reach the highest leaf.

Inky spots

Cut the stalk into slices. Look for inky spots inside. These show where water has risen up the stalk.

Frozen water

When water gets very cold it freezes hard and turns to ice.

Differences

Look at an ice-cube. How is it different from water?

Can you pour ice like water?

Water can change shape because it is a liquid. Ice keeps one shape unless it melts and turns back to water.

Anything that keeps its shape, like ice, is called a solid.

Taking up space

Find a plastic pot with a lid. Fill it with water and put on the lid. Ask if you can put the pot in a freezer. What happens when all the water turns to ice?

Fill up to the brim.

Ice takes up more space than water. It pushes the lid up when it gets too big for the pot.

Does ice float?

Put some ice in a bowl of water to see if it floats.

How much floats above the surface?

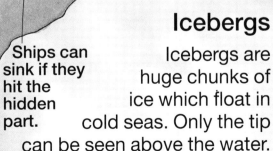

Ships can sink if they hit the hidden part.

Icebergs

Icebergs are huge chunks of ice which float in cold seas. Only the tip can be seen above the water.

20

Melting ice

Ice melts when it gets warmer.

Guess what happens if you put one ice-cube in cold water, one in hot water and one on a plate.

Try this out to see if you are right.

Use a watch to time how fast they melt.

Melting without heating

Try sprinkling an ice-cube with salt.

What happens to the salt?

Try pressing an ice-cube with a spoon-handle.

What happens to the ice here?

Ice always melts when it is pressed.

The salt mixes with the ice. Salty ice melts quickly because it melts at cooler temperatures than plain ice.

Why ice is slippery

Ice melts when your feet press on it. A thin layer of water forms under your shoes. This stops them from gripping so you slide around.

21

Notes for parents and teachers

These notes give more detailed explanations of the scientific topics covered in this part of the book.

Experimenting with water (pages 2-3)

In common with all liquids, water flows, changes shape to fit any container, keeps the same volume and finds its own level.

Floating (pages 4-5)

When an object is dropped in water its bulk pushes some water aside. The water pushes back, exerting a force called upthrust. If an object is heavy its weight may overcome the upthrust so it sinks. If it is light enough, it floats.

It is possible to make something push aside more water by changing its shape. The boat-shaped plasticine pushes aside more water than the ball. This increases the upthrust so it now keeps the plasticine afloat.

Fun with boats (pages 6-7)

A boat sinks into water until it displaces the same weight of water as its own weight. When loaded, the boat sinks lower into the water until it displaces the weight of its cargo as well as its own weight.

Salt water weighs more than fresh water. A boat has to displace less salt water to equal its own weight. This makes it float higher in salt water. It can also carry more.

Water's 'skin' (pages 8-9)

Like all substances, water is made up of tiny particles called molecules. Water molecules hold together most strongly at the surface. This makes it able to resist slight pressure, just like a skin. This effect is known as surface tension.

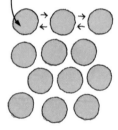

The surface molecules attract each other.

Vanishing water (pages 10-11)

Molecules move constantly in a liquid. They often break free and escape as gas (evaporation). Heat gives molecules more energy so they move faster and break free more easily.

▼

Escaping molecules

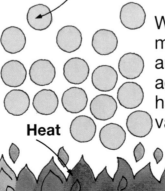

Heat

When a gas cools, its molecules lose energy and can form a liquid again. That is what happens when water vapour condenses.

Mixing (pages 12-13)

Water forms different mixtures with various other substances.

Solutions

A solution is formed when a substance, such as salt, dissolves in water. Its molecules spread out among the water molecules so they are thoroughly mixed.

Suspensions and emulsions

A suspension is formed when a powdery substance, such as fine sand, does not dissolve. Its particles stay large enough to see. They can be easily filtered out.

A liquid, such as oil, that refuses to mix with water can form an emulsion. It stays in droplets suspended in the water.

Water power (pages 14-15)

Water flows downward due to gravity (Earth's pull). The force of its flow is useful for powering machinery.

Its flow is also affected by its depth. The deepest parts of any volume of water are under the most pressure because of the weight of water above.

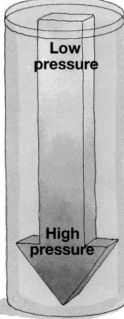

Low pressure

High pressure

Air and water tricks (pages 16-17)

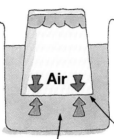

Air

Water

When a glass is pushed underwater, air is trapped inside. The air pressure balances the water pressure outside.

The water compresses the air but cannot push past it.

Taking in water (pages 18-19)

Water molecules can be more attracted to other substances than they are to each other. The attraction enables water to travel a long way into some substances. This is called capillary action.

Capillary action encourages water to climb up plants. Plants allow water to evaporate from their leaves which also helps to 'suck up' the water.

Frozen water (pages 20-21)

When water becomes very cold the molecules lock together to form a solid (ice). Heat gives the molecules energy so they can break free and change to liquid. This also happens if pressure is applied.

Water facts

Here you can find out all sorts of facts about water.

Wet Earth

★ Over 70% of the Earth's surface is covered in water.

Frozen water

★ About three-quarters of the world's fresh water is in the form of ice or snow.

Plants and animals

★ All plants and animals, including people, need water to live and grow. Most are made of about 70% water.

Camels

★ Camels come from hot, dry places. They can drink 23 gallons of water at one time and live on this for three weeks.

Water inside you

★ A fully grown person has about 10 gallons of water inside them.

★ Everyone has to take in about 2 quarts of water a day. People get almost half their water from food.

★ Most people use between 40 and 130 gallons a day for drinking, flushing the toilet, washing, cooking, cleaning and so on.

Going without

★ The longest anyone has survived without water is 18 days.

Making water

★ Scientists can make water from two gases, Hydrogen (H) and Oxygen (O). They call water H_2O after these gases.

Boiling and freezing

★ Water freezes and turns to ice at 0 degrees centigrade. It boils when its temperature reaches 100 degrees centigrade.

SCIENCE WITH MAGNETS

Consultants: Joan and Maurice Martin

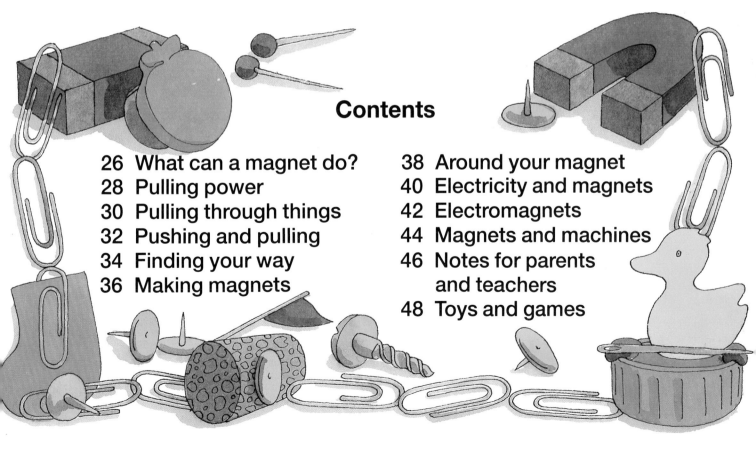

Contents

What can a magnet do?

The experiments and games in this part of the book will help you find out what magnets can do. You can use any magnet for most of the activities but you will need bar magnets for some of them.

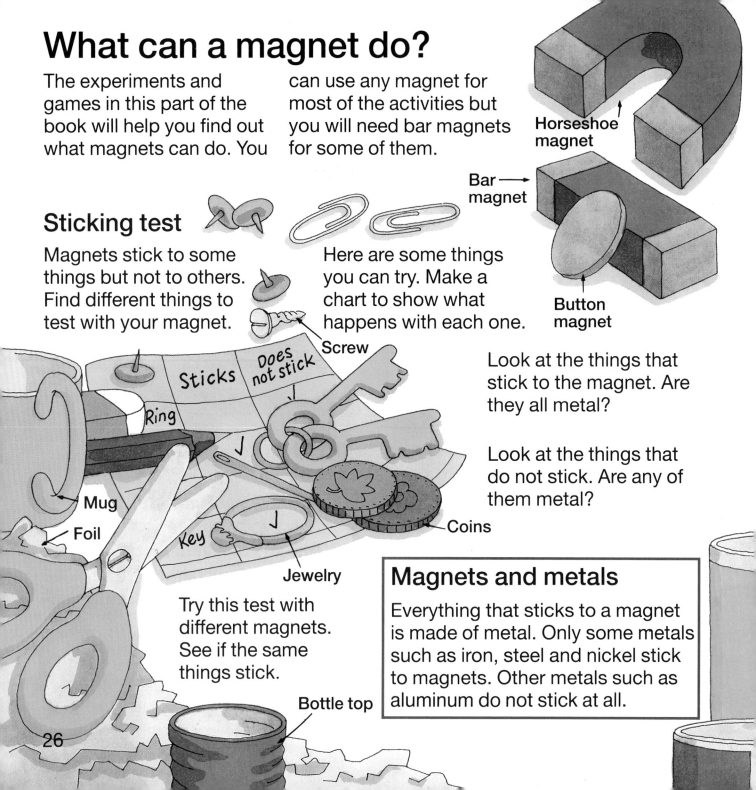

Horseshoe magnet

Bar → magnet

Button magnet

Sticking test

Magnets stick to some things but not to others. Find different things to test with your magnet.

Here are some things you can try. Make a chart to show what happens with each one.

Screw

	Sticks	Does not stick
Ring		
	✓	
Key	✓	
Jewelry	✓	

Mug

Foil

Coins

Look at the things that stick to the magnet. Are they all metal?

Look at the things that do not stick. Are any of them metal?

Try this test with different magnets. See if the same things stick.

Bottle top

Magnets and metals

Everything that sticks to a magnet is made of metal. Only some metals such as iron, steel and nickel stick to magnets. Other metals such as aluminum do not stick at all.

26

Useful magnets

Look around your home to see if you can find magnets being used.

Magnet   Steel plate

Magnets keep some cupboards closed.

Magnetic letters can spell words on metal doors.

Sorting cans

Cans are usually made of aluminum or steel. Try a magnet out on lots of different ones. The ones that do not stick are aluminum.

Old cans are melted so their metal may be used again. Magnets are used to sort the cans so aluminum ones can be melted separately.

Cellophane tape

Matching socks game

Use the sticking power of your magnet to make a game.

You need: 2 magnets, thread, paper, paints or crayons, sticky tape*, scissors, paper-clips, large box.

Cut the paper into sock shapes. Color them in twos so they look like different pairs. Put a paperclip on each one.

Throw the socks into the box. Tape a thread to each magnet. Taking turns with a friend, dip a magnet into the box and pull out a sock.

See who can get the most pairs.

Pulling power

Magnets can pull, or attract, some metal things towards them.

Pulling test

See how far your magnet can pull a pin.

Put a ruler flat on a table.

▲ Place a pin at zero (0) on the ruler.

◄ Put the magnet four inches away. Push it slowly towards the pin. Wait for a few seconds at each mark.

When the pin jumps to the magnet, look at the number beside the magnet. This shows how far the pin has jumped.

This magnet pulls the pin about 1½ inches.

Workers who build things out of steel can get tiny splinters of steel in their eyes. Doctors use a special magnet to pull the splinters out.

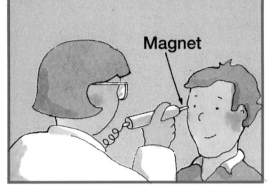

Magnet

Try the same test with as many magnets as you can. See which one can pull the pin furthest.

You could write down your results on a chart like this.

CHAMP

Magnet used	Pulls pin
My magnet	1½ in
Alfie's magnet	¾ in
Fridge magnet	1 in

Chart

Force

Magnets make things move with an invisible pull. This is called magnetic force.

Try pulling a pin off a magnet. Feel the magnetic force pulling back. You have to pull more strongly than the magnet.

Gravity

The Earth tries to pull everything down towards its centre. This pull is called the force of gravity. You have to pull against it when you lift things up.

Pulling upward

Hold the ruler up against the edge of a table so zero is level with the table-top. Put a pin at zero.

Sticky tape helps to keep the ruler upright.

Slide your strongest magnet slowly down the ruler until the pin jumps up. Stop and look at the number beside the magnet.

The magnet cannot pull the pin as far as before. This is because another kind of force is trying to pull the pin down. This is the force of gravity (see above right).

Flying butterfly

Cut a butterfly shape out of some tissue. Slide a paperclip on to it.

Tie one end of a thread to the clip. Tape the other end to a table.

See if you can make the butterfly fly without letting your magnet touch the clip.

The force of gravity tries to pull the clip down.

Pulling through things

Try these experiments to see if you can stop a magnet working.

Blocking test

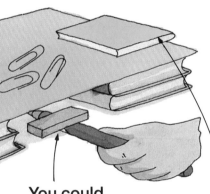

Rest a sheet of paper across two piles of books. Put paperclips on top.

You could tape the magnet on to a pencil.

Rest more books on top to keep the paper still.

Hold a magnet underneath. Can you make it move the clips?

The magnet works through the paper. See if it can work through other things.

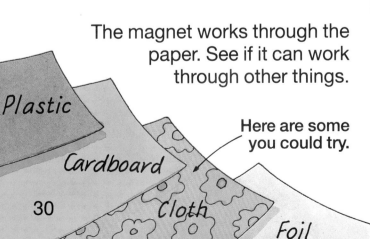

Here are some you could try.

Plastic

Cardboard

Cloth

Foil

30

Sticky metal

Find a metal lid that sticks to a magnet. Put a paperclip on top. See if the magnet can move the clip from under the lid.

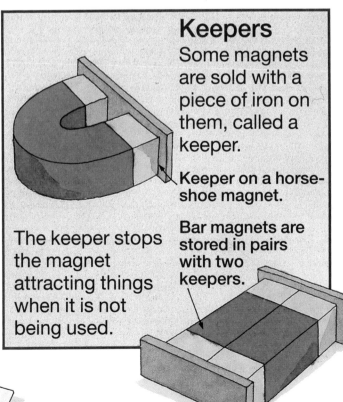

You could use a baking tray instead.

The paperclip is hard to move or may not move at all. This is because the iron or steel in the lid traps the magnet's force.

Keepers

Some magnets are sold with a piece of iron on them, called a keeper.

Keeper on a horse-shoe magnet.

Bar magnets are stored in pairs with two keepers.

The keeper stops the magnet attracting things when it is not being used.

Fun with water

Rest the tray across two piles of magazines. Pour water inside. Push a pin into each cork and put it in the water.

Push the pin in here.

You could pin on paper sails to make the corks look like boats.

Hold the magnet underwater. Can you make it move the corks?

See if you can get all the boats in one corner.

Try using the magnet under the tray as well.

Magnetic holders

Because magnets can work through paper and paint, they can be used to hold up notices on a refrigerator's metal door.

Magnetic puzzle

Put a sheet of paper and a nail on a table. How can you use your magnet to pick up the paper? The experiments on this page should give you a clue.

If you get stuck, turn to the answer on page 74.

Pushing and pulling

These experiments will help you find out more about a magnet's force.

Where is a magnet strongest?

Put a magnet into a box of pins. Lift it out carefully. Where are there most pins? Try this experiment with all sorts of magnets.

A bar shape has most pins at the ends.

A horseshoe magnet has lots of pins at both ends.

This round magnet is strongest on each flat side.

Every magnet has two strong places. These are called poles. They are at opposite ends.

About poles

Both poles pick up pins in the same way. Try this experiment to see if the poles are the same in other ways.

1. Put two bar magnets eight inches apart, so the ends face each other. Push one towards the other. Watch what happens. ▼

Do not hold this one.

Watch how this magnet moves.

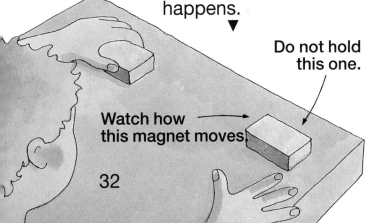

32

◀ 2. Tape colored paper on to the poles (ends) that stick. Use two different colors.

3. Turn both magnets round. Do the other poles also stick? Mark them so each magnet has its poles in different ◀ colors, as shown.

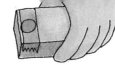

4. Now try to push two of the same-colored poles together. Can you feel them pushing back?

Each magnet has two sorts of pole. One is called north, the other south*. Poles of the same kind push each other away but different poles pull towards each other.

North pole	◄ ►	North pole
North poles push away, or repel, each other.		
South pole	◄ ►	South pole
South poles repel each other.		
North pole		South pole
A north pole and a south pole pull together, or attract.		

Try putting different shaped magnets together. Can you find which poles are the same?

*You can find out more about these on pages 34 and 35.

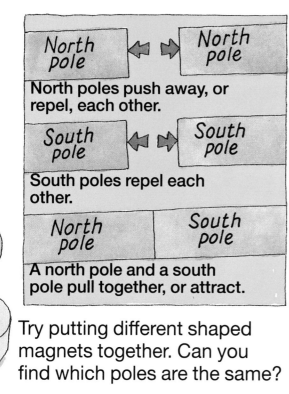

Pushing game

Tape one magnet on to a toy car. Use one pole of another magnet to push the car along.

How fast can you make the car go?

Floating magnets

Use the marked magnets for this trick. First cut some thin strips of sticky tape.

Put a pencil on one magnet. Put the other magnet on top so the same colors are together. ▶ Join the magnets with tape.

Keep the tape loose like this.

Now take the pencil away. The top magnet floats above the bottom magnet.

Try pressing this magnet.

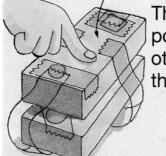

The same-colored poles try to push each other away. This keeps the magnet in the air.

Finding your way

Magnets help sailors, explorers and hikers to find their way. Here you can find out how.

Pointing magnet

Tape a bar magnet into a plastic pot. Float the pot in a bowl of water. Let the pot settle.

Mark the bowl opposite the two ends of the magnet.

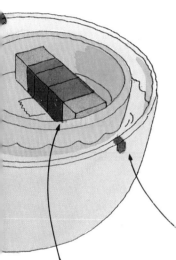

Use a felt-tip pen for the marks.

The magnet turns back to face the same way.

Turn the pot, then let go. What happens?

A magnet always turns to point the same way, if it can swing easily. Its north pole (see page 33) points north. Its south pole points south.

Finding north

The sun always rises in the east and sets in the west. If you get up early and face the sun, north is on your left.

Never look straight at the sun. It can hurt your eyes badly.

Mark the north end of the magnet with a blob of plasticine* or paint.

Make a compass

Card

Cut a circle of cardboard to fit in the pot. Mark east, west, north and south.

Just use the first letters.

When the compass is finished it always shows the right directions.

Put the card in the pot so 'N' is over the north end of the magnet. Then all the arrows will point the right way.

*Plastic modeling clay.

Chinese inventors

The Chinese invented the first compasses. This one had a magnet inside the turtle shape.

The magnet made the turtle turn so its head pointed north.

How a hiker's compass works

A hiker's compass has a magnetic needle. It always points north.

The needle stays still while the card turns.

To find other directions, the hiker turns a card beneath. When N (north) is under the needle all the arrows point the right way.

Another north pole

The north poles of all magnets point to one place. This place is called the Earth's magnetic north pole. It is in the icy, northern Arctic.

Explorers have found that compasses do not work at the Earth's north pole. The magnet inside just spins around.

North Pole

Compass puzzle

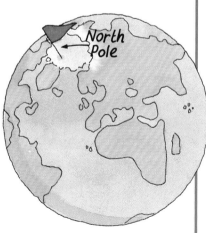

Which way does this hiker have to go to get to the mountains?

Remember the hiker has to turn the compass so 'N' is under the needle.

Answer on page 74.

Making magnets

You can use one magnet to make another. Here are some ways to try this.

Hanging magnets

Hang a nail from the end of a magnet. Try hanging another nail on to the first one. Does it stick?

You can use pins instead of nails.

◀ The first nail is a magnet while it is touching the big magnet. Like all magnets, the nail has two poles.

Magnet's north pole

Nail's north pole

Now hang two nails side by side. Try pushing the pointed ends together. ▶

The ends have the same poles so they push each other away.

A lasting magnet

Stroke one pole of a magnet along a needle. Then lift the magnet away. Repeat 12 times.

The needle becomes a lasting magnet. See how many pins it can pick up.

Stroke the same way each time.

Inside a magnet

A magnet is made of many tiny parts called domains. Each one is like a mini-magnet. They all line up and point the same way.

Any metal that sticks to a magnet also has domains. These are jumbled up. A magnet can make them line up. Then the metal becomes a magnet.

Domains

Domains in an ordinary needle

Domains in a magnetized needle

Magnetic rock

A rock called magnetite is a natural magnet. It was first found at a place called Magnesia. All magnets get their name from this place.

Can you spoil a magnet?

Drop a magnetized needle on a table. Do this a few times. Then see if the needle can pick up pins.

What happens

The domains are shaken out of line so the needle stops being a magnet. Take care not to hit or drop your magnets in case they get spoiled in the same way.

Swimming ducks

You need:
2 needles,
magnet,
plastic
bottle tops,
plasticine,
paper,
scissors.

Magnetize two needles with your magnet. Stroke them both from the eye to the point.

Both needles will have the same poles at the same ends.

◄ Use plasticine to stick each one to a bottle top. Cut out duck shapes and stick them on top.

Stick one duck so its beak is over the needle's eye. Stick the other so its beak is over the point.

Float the bottle tops in water. The ducks seem to swim towards each other. ▼

These ends have different poles so they attract each other.

Around your magnet

Try these experiments so you can find out more about the forces around your magnet.

Magnetic field

Magnetic force works above and below a magnet as well as at its sides.

Magnet patterns

Put a magnet under some cardboard. Sprinkle iron filings on top. Tap it lightly. What happens?

Sprinkle the filings evenly.

The magnet pulls the filings into a pattern around it. This shows that a magnet's force works all round, although it is strongest at the poles.

Pattern made by a bar magnet.

Pattern made by a horseshoe magnet.

Using iron filings

Iron filings are tiny pieces of iron. Ask an adult to make some by filing an iron nail.

Chemistry sets often have iron filings in tubes like this.

Travelling needle

You need:
needle,
slice of cork,
bar magnet,
plasticine,
bowl of
water, sticky
tape.

Magnetize a needle by stroking it with the south pole of a magnet. Stroke the needle 12 times from the eye to the point.

The point will have a north pole.

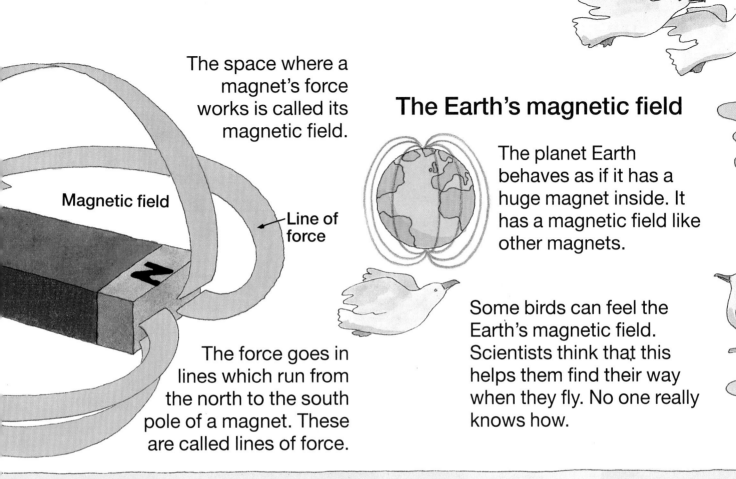

The space where a magnet's force works is called its magnetic field.

Magnetic field

Line of force

N

The force goes in lines which run from the north to the south pole of a magnet. These are called lines of force.

The Earth's magnetic field

The planet Earth behaves as if it has a huge magnet inside. It has a magnetic field like other magnets.

Some birds can feel the Earth's magnetic field. Scientists think that this helps them find their way when they fly. No one really knows how.

Push the needle through the cork. Float it in the water so the point is on top.

Be careful with sharp things.

Stick plasticine under the cork so it floats upright.

Tape the magnet inside the bowl. Move the needle near to the magnet's north pole. Then let go.

The needle floats round to the south pole. It follows a line of force in the magnetic field.*

*Re-magnetize the needle if you want to try this again.

Tape the magnet well above the water.

39

Electricity and magnets

Electricity can act like a magnet. Here you can find out how.

What is electricity?

Electricity is caused by tiny invisible things called electrons. These move easily through metal. Their flow is called an electric current.

Electric surprise

You need: 4.5 volt battery, a 2 in piece of straw, needle, sticky tape, scissors, 60 in of plastic coated wire.

1. Ask an adult to help you cut off the plastic at each end of the wire. Tape one end on to a terminal on the battery.

Terminal

Danger

Only use batteries for experiments. Never use electricity from plugs and sockets. This is too strong and is dangerous.

Electrons flow along metal wires.

Trim the ends of the straw.

Use tape to hold the turns together.

2. Wind the wire on to the straw ◄ to make a coil. Wind on three layers of wire.

3. Tape the free end of the wire to the second terminal. Hold the needle lightly just inside the coil. What happens?

When both terminals are joined, a current flows through the wire.

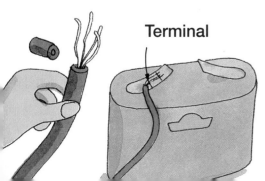

4. The needle is pulled inside ▶ the coil. This is because an electric current has a magnetic field. The coil makes the field strong enough to attract the needle.

This coil is called a solenoid.

Your battery will quickly run down if you leave the solenoid on for long. Switch it off by taking one wire off a terminal.

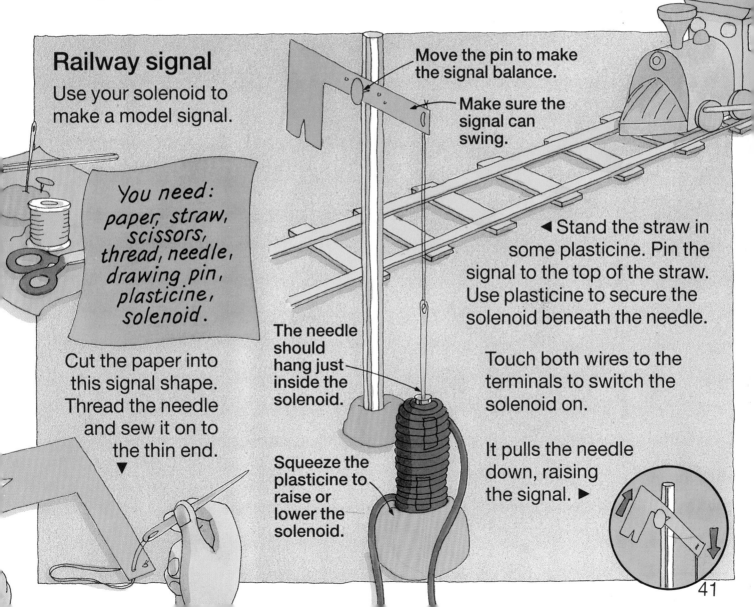

Railway signal

Use your solenoid to make a model signal.

You need:
paper, straw, scissors, thread, needle, drawing pin, plasticine, solenoid.

Cut the paper into this signal shape. Thread the needle and sew it on to the thin end. ▼

Move the pin to make the signal balance.

Make sure the signal can swing.

◀ Stand the straw in some plasticine. Pin the signal to the top of the straw. Use plasticine to secure the solenoid beneath the needle.

The needle should hang just inside the solenoid.

Squeeze the plasticine to raise or lower the solenoid.

Touch both wires to the terminals to switch the solenoid on.

It pulls the needle down, raising the signal. ▶

41

Electromagnets

Some magnets use electricity to make them work. These are called electromagnets.

Making an electromagnet

You can turn the solenoid on page 40 into an electromagnet. Just put a long iron or steel nail inside the straw. Then tape both wires to the battery.
▼

You can rewind the wire around the nail if the nail does not fit in the straw.

Now see if your ▶ electromagnet picks up the same things as other magnets.

Try pins, paperclips and nails.

Magnetic cranes

Some cranes use electromagnets to pick up iron and steel. These magnets are very strong.

The driver switches this magnet off to make the crane drop its load. ➡

Why the electromagnet works

The metal inside the solenoid strengthens its magnetic field. This makes a strong magnet.

Switching off

Now take one end of the wire away from the battery to stop the current. See if paperclips still stick. ▶

The electromagnet stops working because the magnetic field leaves the wire when the current stops flowing*.

*If the nail inside is still magnetic, turn to page 47 to find out why.

Making a toy crane

You can use an electro-magnet to make a crane.

You also need: a spool, a short piece of straw, scissors, a short pencil, a short ruler, a small box, sticky tape, plasticine, 20in of thread.

1. Tape the ruler inside the box, as shown. Stick the spool behind it with plasticine. Push the pencil into the spool, point downwards.

One end of a spool has a notch. This goes on top.

Add tape to keep the spool steady.

2. Tape the straw on to the ruler. Push the thread through the straw. Tie one end to the electromagnet. Tape the other end to the pencil, leaving a tail. ▼

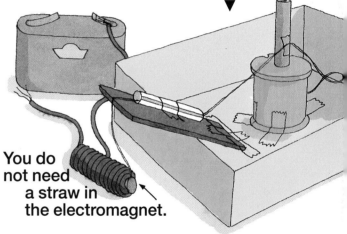

You do not need a straw in the electromagnet.

3. Put the battery inside the box. Tape both wires to the terminals when you want to pick up a load. Turn the pencil to wind the electromagnet up. ▼

Pull one wire off the terminal when you want to drop a load.

Push the tail into the notch to stop the thread unwinding.

You could stick everything into a truck, instead of a box, to make a mobile crane.

Magnets and machines

Magnets help to make many electric machines work. Here you can find out about some of them.

Magnet

Coil of wire spins.

Magnet

Making electricity

A machine called an electric generator is used to make electricity. The generator has a coil of wire with magnets around it.

Electric generator

This rod turns.

A rod turns the coil of wire in between the magnets. When the coil turns in the magnetic field, electricity flows through the wire.

An electric motor

An electric motor has a coil of wire and magnets like a generator but works the other way round. The coil is still until electricity flows into it from a battery. The flow of electricity in between the magnets makes the coil spin.

Axle

Rod

Here you can see how an electric motor turns the wheels in a toy car.

An electric motor in a toy car

Axle

Coil of wire

Magnets

The spinning coil makes this rod turn round and round.

The rod makes the wheels turn, so the car moves along.

Tape recorders

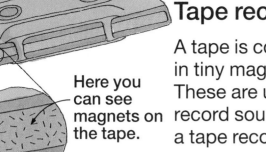

Here you can see magnets on the tape.

A tape is covered in tiny magnets. These are used to record sounds in a tape recorder.

When someone speaks into a microphone, it changes the sound into electrical signals.

Microphone

Tape recorder

Signals go along this wire.

The signals go to an electromagnet. This arranges the magnets on the tape in a pattern to match the signals. ▶

The electromagnet is called a recording head.

This pattern stays on the tape to record the sound.

When you play the tape it moves past a different electromagnet, called a playback head. The pattern makes this head give off electrical signals. ▶

Play-back head

These are the same as the signals made when the sound was recorded. They go to a loudspeaker which uses them to make the sound again.

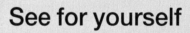
Loudspeaker ▼

See for yourself

Try wiping a magnet along an old tape that no one wants. Then play the tape.

Turn the reels with a pencil.

The tape will not work properly. This is because the magnet has destroyed the pattern that recorded the sound.

Notes for parents and teachers

These notes are intended to help answer any questions that arise from the activities on earlier pages.

Pulling power (pages 28-29)

A strong magnet can affect an object at a greater distance than a weaker one. It is said to have a stronger magnetic field (see page 38).

Gravity

All planets pull things towards their center. This pull, or gravitational force, makes things feel heavy when you lift them. If it did not act, everything on the planet would become weightless and float around.

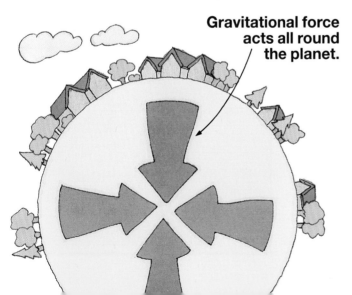

Gravitational force acts all round the planet.

Pulling through things (pages 30-31)

Magnetic force is almost unaffected by things a magnet does not attract. It works as well through a sheet of paper as it does through air. A thick wad of paper may seem to stop a magnet working. But this is simply because the depth of paper keeps objects out of the magnet's field. However, even a thin sheet of iron, steel or nickel does interfere with a magnet's field.

Keepers

Iron keepers trap the magnetic field so there are no free poles (see page 32) to attract other objects. This closed circuit helps to keep the field strong.

Direction of magnetic field

Pushing and pulling (pages 32-33)

Every type and shape of magnet has two kinds of pole; north and south. In every case, unlike poles attract; like ones repel each other.

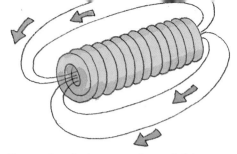

Finding your way (pages 34-35)

The Earth's magnetic field (see page 39) acts as if it has a south pole in the Arctic. This attracts the north poles of all magnets. The place where they point is confusingly known as the magnetic north pole.

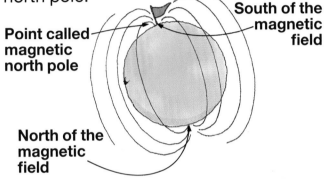

Point called magnetic north pole

South of the magnetic field

North of the magnetic field

Making magnets (pages 36-37)

Different magnetic metals have different qualities. Soft iron is easy to magnetize but also loses its magnetism easily. Steel is harder to magnetize but keeps its magnetism unless hammered or heated.

Electricity and magnets (pages 40-41)

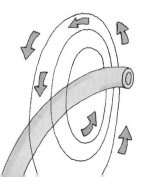

A current flowing in a wire produces a magnetic field in a pattern of concentric circles. A large current has a strong field.

Coiling the wire into a solenoid increases the amount of current-carrying wire. It also creates a magnetic field like that of a bar magnet.

Wires to use

Plastic-coated wire works well and can be bought from any electrical shop. Glazed copper wire gives even better results but is more difficult to find.

Plastic-coated wire

Electromagnets (pages 42-43)

Copper wire

Core

An iron or steel core strengthens the magnetic field of a solenoid. This makes a strong magnet. An electromagnet can be made even stronger by making more turns of the wire or increasing the current.

The core may stay magnetic even when the current is turned off. This depends on the type of metal. Industrial electromagnets use soft iron which does not stay magnetic (see above left).

47

Toys and games

See if you can think up ways to use your magnet to make toys and games. Here are some ideas to start you off.

Magnetic puppets

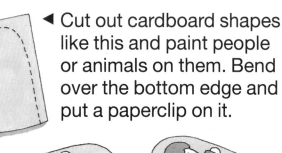

◀ Cut out cardboard shapes like this and paint people or animals on them. Bend over the bottom edge and put a paperclip on it.

Cut out one side of a shoe box. Then turn the box upside down and put the puppets on top. ▼

Tape your magnet to a pencil. Move the magnet inside the box to make the puppets move.

Magic walnut

Ask an adult to help you shell a walnut so the shell stays in two halves. Tape a magnet in one half. Then glue the shell together.

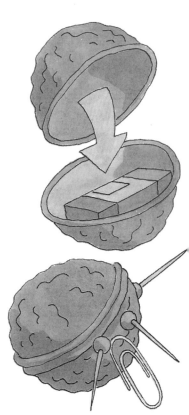

You now have a walnut which seems to pick up pins by magic.

Magnetic pick-up-sticks

Use cocktail sticks for this game. Push a paper-clip on to each one, as shown. ▶

Drop the sticks in a pile. Use your magnet to try to pick one out at a time, without moving any of the others.

SCIENCE WITH
LIGHT
& MIRRORS

Consultant: John Baker (Primary Science Adviser)

Contents

Light all around

Light is all around you. Try the experiments in this book to find out more about light and the different ways it behaves.

Moving light

You need a flashlight for some of the experiments. Switch one on in a dark room.

The light travels away from the flashlight.

See how the flashlight lights up things on the other side of the room.

Anything that makes light is called a light source. Light travels from its source to light things up far away.

Sunlight

The Sun is a ball of burning hot gases. It gives off a very bright light. This travels a distance of 150 million km (93.2 million miles) to reach the Earth.

Making light

How many things can you think of that make light? Here are some to start you off.

Light moves away from a light bulb to light up a room.

Car headlights can light up the road for a long way ahead.

Speedy light

Light is the fastest thing in the universe. It moves at 300,000 km (186,451 miles) a second. It takes only eight and a half minutes to reach Earth from the Sun.

Passing through

Collect some things to test whether light can travel through them or not. Here are some you can try. ▶

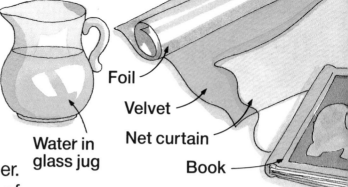

Water in glass jug

Foil

Velvet

Net curtain

Book

Point a flashlight at some paper. Hold each thing in front of the flashlight. Try to guess if it will let light through on to the paper.

Switch on the flashlight to see if you are right. Make a chart to show what happens with the different things.

You could make your chart like this. ⌐

	LIGHT GOES THROUGH	NO LIGHT GOES THROUGH
FOIL	X	✓
TISSUE PAPER	✓	X

Different names

Clear things that let light through are called transparent. Things that stop light are called opaque. Some things let light through even though you cannot see through them. These are called translucent.

Which comes first?

Thunderclouds make lightning and a rumble of thunder at the same time.

You see lightning before you hear thunder because light travels faster than sound.

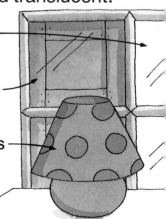

Glass windows are transparent.

Wooden shutters are opaque.

Most lampshades are translucent.

Travelling light

Although you cannot see it, light is always moving. Here you can find out more about how it travels.

Aiming light

Cover the end of a flashlight with foil. Make a hole with a pencil so a thin beam of light can shine through.

Push the pencil through the middle of the foil.

Move the flashlight around. Can you make the beam hit anything you want?

It is easy to aim the beam because the light goes in a straight line.

In the spotlight

Because light travels in straight lines, strong light from theater spotlights can be aimed at actors on a stage.

Rays

Each tiny part of light goes along a straight line. These lines are called rays.

This picture shows how rays travel away from a light source.

Bouncing light

Put the foil-covered flashlight on a table in a dark room. Hold a mirror in front of it. What happens to the beam of light?

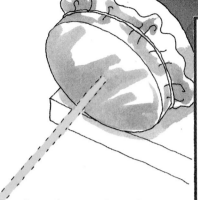

Look out for the light spot at the end of the beam. Is it where you expect?

When light hits things, it can bounce off them and travel in a different direction.

You could try using foil or a shiny tin lid instead of a mirror.

Light spot

Try moving the mirror. Can you make the light spot hit different things in the room?

Why is night dark?

The Earth is like a huge ball. It spins around once every 24 hours. For some of the time your part of the Earth faces the Sun and so it is light.

Here it is night.

Here it is daytime.

The sunlight cannot bend around the Earth, so the other side is dark.

How you see

Some light bounces off all the things you see. The light carries a picture of each thing to your eyes.

Light goes to this toy car.

Light rays carry a picture of the car to your eyes.

Looking in mirrors

When you look in a mirror you see your own face. The picture in the mirror is called a reflection.

Finding reflections

Find all sorts of things that you can see your face in. What do you notice about them?

Saucepan

Spoon

Feel each one to find out if it is rough or smooth. Do all the things look shiny?

Aluminum foil

Glass

See if your reflection looks the same in all of them. Is it always the same shape?

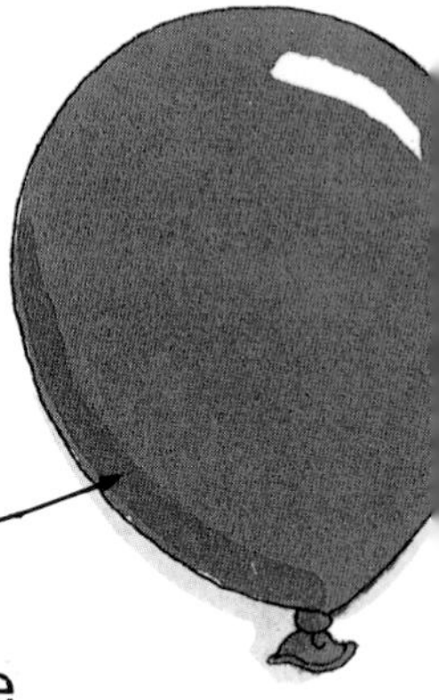

New balloon

Seeing a reflection

You see a reflection when light rays bounce off something and on to a mirror.

Light rays

The light rays bounce off the mirror and into your eyes. This makes you see the reflection.

You see the best reflections in things that are flat, shiny and smooth. These make good mirrors.

Reflections in water

Look at a puddle on a calm day. It gives a good reflection.

Drop a small pebble in to make ripples in the water. What happens to the reflection?

The light bounces off the ripples in all directions. This makes the reflection disappear.

Glass mirrors

Many mirrors are made of glass. They have a thin layer of silver or aluminum under the glass.

Lots of light bounces off this shiny layer so the mirror gives a good reflection.

Make an unbreakable mirror

You can use this unbreakable mirror for many of the experiments in this book.

Cut out rectangles from the foil, the cardboard and the plastic.

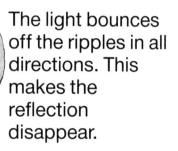

Plastic
Foil
Cardboard

Keep the foil smooth.

Make the rectangles all the same size.

You need:
stiff clear plastic*,
aluminum foil,
stiff cardboard,
scissors,
cellophane tape

Put the foil on the cardboard, shiniest side up. Then put the plastic on top.

Put a thin band of tape around the edges to finish it.

* You could use a clear plastic lid from a food container.

Reflections

You do not always see what you expect to when you look in a mirror. Reflections often look different from real things.

You and your reflection

Look at your reflection in a large mirror. Hold up your left hand.

Watch what happens in the mirror. It's easier if you stand slightly sideways.

Your reflection holds up its right hand. Reflections are always the wrong way around like this. Try other movements to see what happens in the mirror.

Mirror magic

Draw half a circle. Put a mirror along the straight edge.

The mirror shows the half circle back-to-front so it looks like the other half of the circle.

Place your mirror on the dotted lines to complete these three pictures.

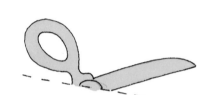

Can you draw halves of other things that you can complete with a mirror?

This only works with things that split into two halves exactly the same. Things like this are called symmetrical.

A butterfly is symmetrical.

Funny reflections

Find a large, shiny spoon that can act like a mirror. Look at your face in the back of it.

Mirrors that curve outwards like this are called convex.

Mirrors that curve inwards like this are called concave.

Is the reflection the same shape as in a flat mirror?

Now turn the spoon over. What happens to your reflection? Does it change if you bring the spoon closer to your face?

Is the reflection always the same way up?

Trick mirrors

Funfairs often use curved mirrors to make people look a funny shape.

Curved mirrors change a reflection's shape. Some can even turn a reflection upside-down.

Secret code writing

This secret code can only be read in a mirror.

Plain paper

Carbon paper

meet me at midnight.

Lay the carbon paper inky side up. Put plain paper over it. 'Write' on top with the needle.

The message appears back-to-front on the other side of the paper.

Use a mirror to turn the message around so anyone can read it.

You need: a mirror, carbon paper, paper, a knitting needle.

meet me at midnight!

Changing reflections

See what happens to the reflections if you use more than one mirror.

Endless reflections

Put two mirrors face to face and tape them together.

Put tape down one edge only.

Stand the mirrors up and put something small in between. How many reflections can you see?

Now move the mirrors closer together. Watch the reflections. ▶

As the mirrors close, the light bounces from one to the other and back again. You see reflections of reflections.

You see most reflections if you untape the mirrors and hold them face to face either side of the object.

Can you count all the reflections you see? —

Count the reflections now.

Making shapes

Tape the mirrors together again. Put a pencil in front of them. Can you make its reflection form different shapes?

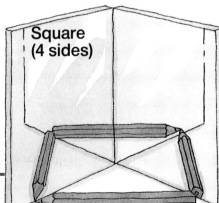

Square (4 sides)

Open or close the mirrors to make these shapes.

Triangle
(3 sides)

Pentagon
(5 sides)

Hexagon
(6 sides)

Make a kaleidoscope

Kaleidoscopes use reflections to make colorful patterns.

Tape the long sides of the mirrors together. ▶

The mirrors face each other.

You will need:
3 rectangular mirrors the same size,
clear plastic,   cardboard,
tracing paper,   scissors,
cellophane tape,   a colored pencil,
colored paper cut into tiny shapes.

◀ Stand the mirrors up on some cardboard. Draw around them and cut out the shape.

Tape two sides of these together to make an envelope. Put the colored paper inside. ▶

You only need a few pieces.

Tape the cardboard to the mirrors. Push a pencil in the middle to make a hole. ▶

Peephole

◀ Tape up the third side and stick the envelope to the open end of the mirrors.

The tracing paper goes on the outside.

Plastic

Tracing paper

◀ Draw around the mirrors on the plastic and tracing paper. Cut out the shapes.

Point this end to the light and look through the peephole. ▶

The mirrors reflect the shapes in a pattern. It changes when you shake the kaleidoscope. ▶

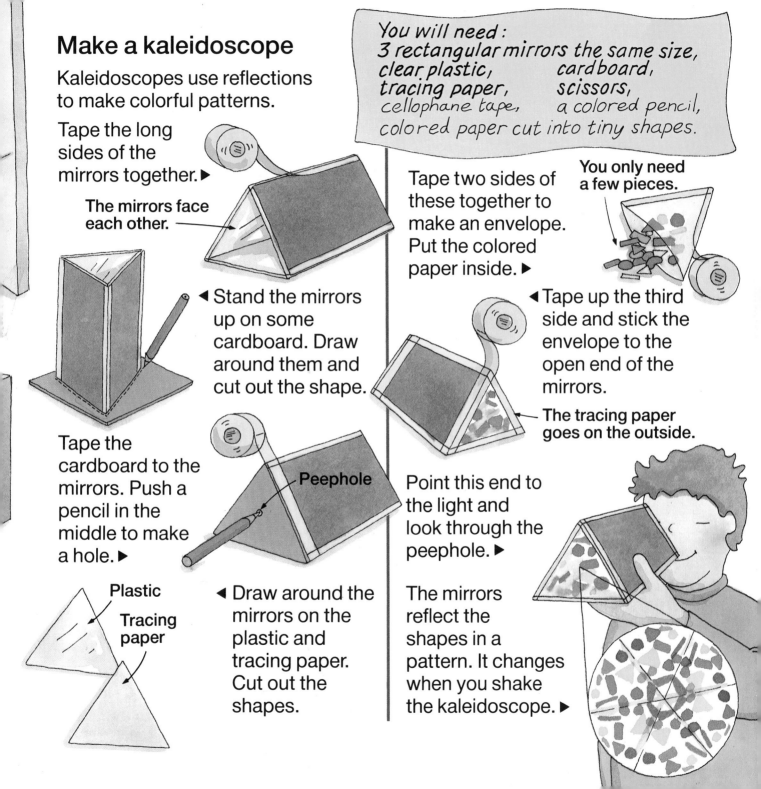

Looking around

Mirrors can help you see things around corners and in awkward places. Here you can find out how.

Looking behind

Hold a mirror in front of you. Can you see anything besides your reflection?

Try moving the mirror slightly to one side.

You can see things behind you because light bounces off them and on to the mirror.

Ask a friend to move around behind you. Can you keep her reflection in the mirror?

You have to tilt the mirror to see your friend in different places.

Make a periscope

This shows you how to use mirrors to make a periscope.

You need:
a long, thin cardboard box,
2 small mirrors the same size,
scissors,
cellophane tape.

1. Ask an adult to cut matching slits in two opposite sides of the box, as shown. Do this near the top and the bottom.

The slits must slant like this.

Useful mirrors

Drivers use mirrors to help them see other traffic on the road behind them.

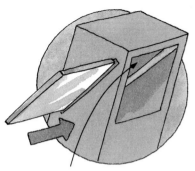

Cut the window in the side nearest the top of the slits.

◀ 2. Cut a window level with the top slits. Slide a mirror through the slits so the shiny side faces the window. Tape it in place.

3. Cut another ▶ window on the opposite side of the box, level with the bottom slits. Slide a second mirror through the slits and fasten it with tape.

The shiny side of the mirror faces the window.

4. Point the periscope over a wall and look through the bottom window. What can you see?

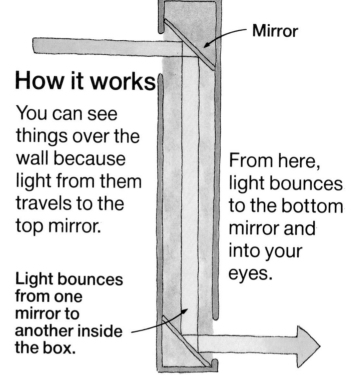

Mirror

How it works

You can see things over the wall because light from them travels to the top mirror.

Light bounces from one mirror to another inside the box.

From here, light bounces to the bottom mirror and into your eyes.

Up periscope

The crew of a submarine can see what is happening above the surface by raising a periscope out of the water.

The light carries pictures down to the crew.

Tricks of light

Light can play some surprising tricks on your eyes. You cannot always believe what you see.

Straight or bent?

Put a straw in a glass of water. Look down on it from above. What happens to the straw?

The straw looks bent at the surface of the water.

Try other straight things to see if they look bent too.

Light travels more slowly through water than through air. As it slows down, it changes direction. This can make things in water look bent when they are really straight.

Appearing coin

Stick a coin to the bottom of a bowl with tape. Look over the edge of the bowl, then move back until you just cannot see the coin anymore.

Keep still and ask a friend to pour water into the bowl. What happens?

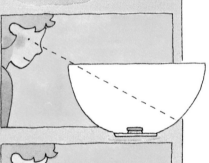

When the bowl is empty, the edge of the bowl stops you seeing the coin.

When the bowl is full, the light bends over the edge so you can see the coin.

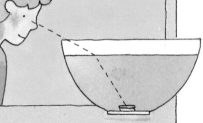

Changing shape

Collect some things that you can see through. Hold them in front of a book. What happens to the words?

Try some of these things.

The words look a different shape because light bends when it passes through any clear object.

Ruler

Ice

Marble

The amount it bends depends on the shape of the object.

Pair of glasses

Fill a clean glass jar with water and stand it in front of the page.

The words look bigger through the jar.

The jar and the water make a solid curved shape. This shape bends the light to make the words look bigger. This is called magnification.

In the swim

A swimming pool looks shallower than it really is because of the way light is bent through water. This also makes your legs look short and fat.

Magnifying glass

A magnifier is made of a piece of solid curved glass called a lens. The lens makes light bend just as a jar of water does.

This lens has been cut in half so you can see how it is curved.

Microscope

Lenses are used in microscopes to make tiny things look many times bigger.

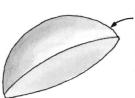

Making pictures

Photographs are pictures made by light rays. Here you can find out how light can make pictures and how light helps you to see pictures too.

Make a pinhole camera

Light can make pictures appear for a moment inside this camera.

Cut out the top of the box, then paint the inside black. Let the paint dry. Tape tracing paper over the opening.

You need:
a cardboard box,
black paint and a paintbrush.
tracing paper,
cellophane tape, scissors,
a pin,
a dark cloth.

The pictures will appear on this tracing paper screen.

Use a pin to push a tiny hole in the box, opposite the tracing paper screen.

Hole

Go outside. Hold the screen up to your eyes. Ask a friend to put a cloth over your head and around the sides of the box.

Point the hole at different things to get a picture on the screen. Do you notice anything surprising?

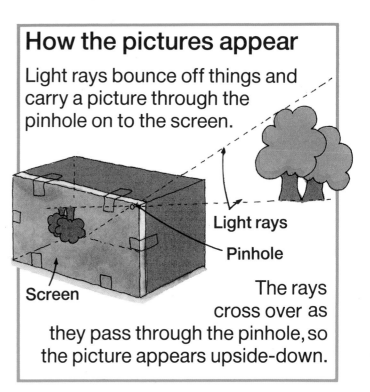

How the pictures appear

Light rays bounce off things and carry a picture through the pinhole on to the screen.

Light rays

Pinhole

Screen

The rays cross over as they pass through the pinhole, so the picture appears upside-down.

Taking photographs

Real cameras have film at the back instead of a screen.

When you press a button, a shutter lets light in. The light marks a picture on the film. This can be printed on to paper to make a photograph.

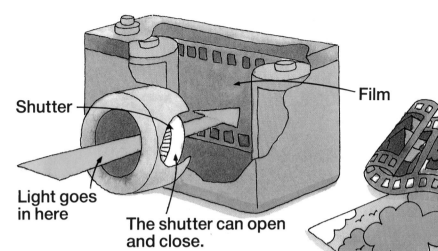

Shutter

Film

Light goes in here

The shutter can open and close.

How your eyes see pictures

Your eyes work a little like a pinhole camera. A hole at the front, called the pupil, lets light in.

The light carries a picture to the back of your eye. This part is called the retina.

This shows the inside of your eye.

Retina

Pupil

The picture is upside-down. Your brain turns it around so that you see things the right way up.

Looking at eyes

Stand in a dim room for a few minutes and look at your eyes in a mirror. Look closely at your pupils. Then put the light on. See how your pupils change size.

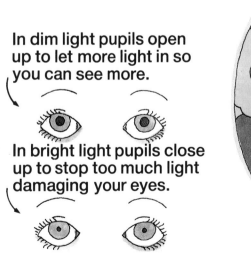

In dim light pupils open up to let more light in so you can see more.

In bright light pupils close up to stop too much light damaging your eyes.

The color of light

Most light looks clear or white, but it is really a mixture of different colors.

Make your own rainbow

You can make the different colors appear like this.

Stand with your back to the Sun and spray water from a hose. What colors can you see in the spray?

Look into the spray against a dark wall or hedge.

Color wheel

You can make colors change with this spinning color wheel.

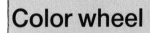

You need: cardboard, a jar, colored crayons, scissors, a pencil, ruler.

Draw around the bottom of a jar to make a circle. Cut the circle out.

Rainbow colors

A rainbow appears in the sky when the Sun shines through rain. The same colors always appear in the same order.

Violet
Indigo
Blue
Green
Yellow
Orange
Red

Light bends as it goes through the water. Each color of light bends by a different amount so you see each one separately. The bands of colored light make a rainbow.

Follow this as a guide.

Divide the circle into seven roughly equal parts. Color each part a different rainbow color.

Push a sharp pencil through the middle of the circle. Spin it quickly on a table. Watch what happens to the colors on the card.

Different colors of light bounce off each part of the wheel. As the wheel spins, these merge to make one very pale color.

Colored things

Most things only let some colors of light bounce off them. You see the colors as they bounce off.

This red pepper looks red because only red light bounces off it.

If all the colors bounce off something, you see them mixed together. This mixture looks white.

This hanky looks white because all the colors bounce off it.

Changing color

Collect some see-through wrappers in different colors. Look at some white paper through each one. Does the paper always look white?

All the colors of light bounce off the paper, but each wrappers only lets its own color through. This makes the paper look the same color as the wrapper.

Light and shadow

Whenever there is light, things have shadows. Here you can find out how shadows happen.

This works best in a dark room.

Is the shadow always the same shape and size as your hand?

Making shadows

Put a flashlight on a chair and shine it at a wall. Put your hand in front. What do you see on the wall?

A shadow shows where your hand blocks the light and stops it reaching the wall.

Make different shapes with your hand. See what happens to the shadow.

Sun shadows

Things outside have shadows because they keep sunlight from reaching the ground.

Go outside with a friend on a sunny day. Measure each other's shadows at different times. Does your shadow stay the same length?

When the Sun is high you only block out a few rays of light so your shadow is short.

When the Sun is low you block out more rays of light and so your shadow is long.

All shadows are short at midday, when the Sun is high in the sky.

Shadows are longer in the morning and evening, when the Sun is low.

Make a shadow theater

Cut the top and bottom out of a cardboard box. Cut a slot in each side, as shown. ▶

Slots

Give your shadow show in a dark room.

◀ Cut out cardboard shapes for puppets. Tape each one to a ruler.

Tape tracing paper over one end of ▶ the box. Push the puppets through the slots. Shine a light behind the puppets to make their shadows appear.

Move the puppets to make the shadows act out a story.

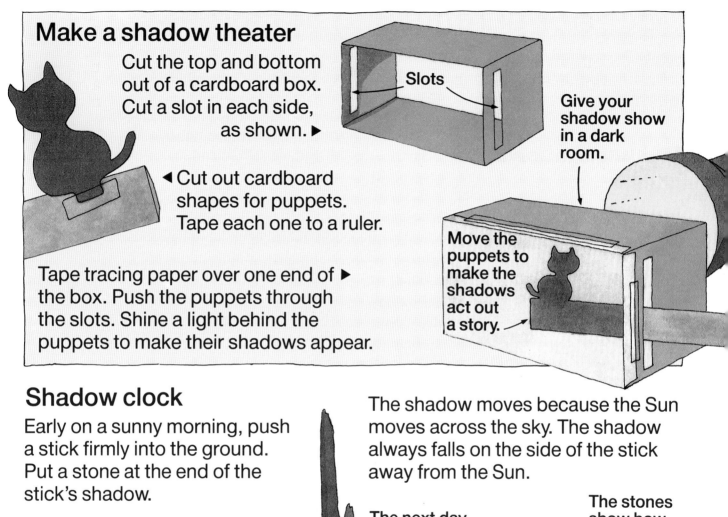

Shadow clock

Early on a sunny morning, push a stick firmly into the ground. Put a stone at the end of the stick's shadow.

Chalk the time on the stone.

See where the shadow is after an hour. Mark the shadow again with another stone. Do this every hour until late afternoon.

The shadow moves because the Sun moves across the sky. The shadow always falls on the side of the stick away from the Sun.

The next day you can tell the time by seeing which stone the shadow is on.

The stones show how the shadow moves.

69

Notes for parents and teachers

These notes are intended to help answer any questions that arise from the activities on earlier pages.

Traveling light (pages 52-53)

Light rays are given off from all light sources. They spread out as they go. Objects further away from a source are less brightly lit than those close to it because fewer rays hit the same surface area.

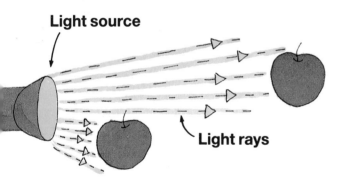

Light source

Light rays

Safety with mirrors

It is safer to put tape around the edges and across the back of a glass mirror. This stops pieces of glass from scattering if a child should break a mirror.

Reflections (pages 56-57)

The way light rays bounce off a mirror affects the way you see the image, or reflection, in the mirror.

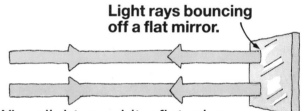

Light rays bouncing off a flat mirror.

When light rays hit a flat mirror head on, they bounce straight back. The image looks the same size as the object.

When light rays hit a concave mirror they bounce inward so they cross. This makes the image look upside-down, unless you are very close to the mirror.

Light rays bouncing off a concave mirror.

A convex mirror makes light rays bounce outward. This makes the image look smaller than the real object.

Light rays bouncing off a convex mirror.

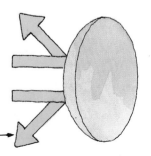

Changing reflections (pages 58-59)

The smaller the angle between two mirrors, the more light can bounce between them. This results in more reflections. In theory, you can see an infinite number of reflections from a point between two parallel mirrors. In real life, this is impossible because you cannot stand between the mirrors without getting in the way of the reflected light.

Tricks of light (62-63)

The way light rays change direction as they travel from one material (such as air or water) to another is known as refraction.

Magnifiers

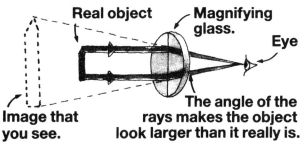

Real object
Magnifying glass.
Eye
Image that you see.
The angle of the rays makes the object look larger than it really is.

Rays of light reflected from an object are bent inward as they go through a magnifying lens. The angle of the rays traveling into your eye causes the image (the picture you see) to look bigger than the object.

Making pictures (pages 64-65)

The picture inside the pinhole camera may be blurred because the rays from a particular point of an object do not hit the screen at the same place. In modern cameras (and in the human eye) a lens bends the light so rays coming from any one point on the object meet to form a clear image.

Lens
Light rays

The color of light (pages 66-67)

Different colors of light bounce off different parts of the spinner. As it turns, they mix into one color. This looks near-white, not pure white, because the crayon colors on the spinner are not exactly the same as those of light.

Light and shadow (pages 68-69)

The shadow clock only tells the time accurately for a few days. This is because the relative positions of the Earth and the Sun slowly change throughout the year. This gradually changes the place where the shadow falls at a given time.

Fun with light and mirrors

You can use light and mirrors for all sorts of tricks, puzzles and games.

Here are some for you to try out with your friends.

In the cage

Draw a lion on one side of a small piece of cardboard.

Draw a cage on the other side. Attach the cardboard to the top of a pencil with sticky tape.

Twist the pencil backward and forward quickly between your hands.

The lion appears in the cage.

The light bounces off the pictures so quickly that you see them mixed together.

Mirror maze

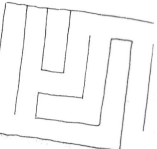

Draw a maze like this one on a piece of paper.

Put the paper on a table. Prop up a mirror behind it so you can see the maze reflected in the mirror.

Put a book in front so you cannot see the paper.

Now, looking only at the reflection, try to draw through the maze from start to finish.

Because things are back to front in mirrors, this is not as easy as it looks.

Index

Answers to puzzles

Page 31 - Put the nail under the paper. Then put your magnet on top. The magnet sticks to the nail through the paper.

The paper is now squashed between the nail and the magnet so you can lift it up by raising the magnet.

Page 35 - The hiker has to go north to get to the mountains.

First published in 1992 by Usborne Publishing Ltd, Usborne House, 83-85 Saffron Hill, London EC1N 8RT, England. www.usborne.com